A Picr

by Linda Koons • illustrated

MW01101418

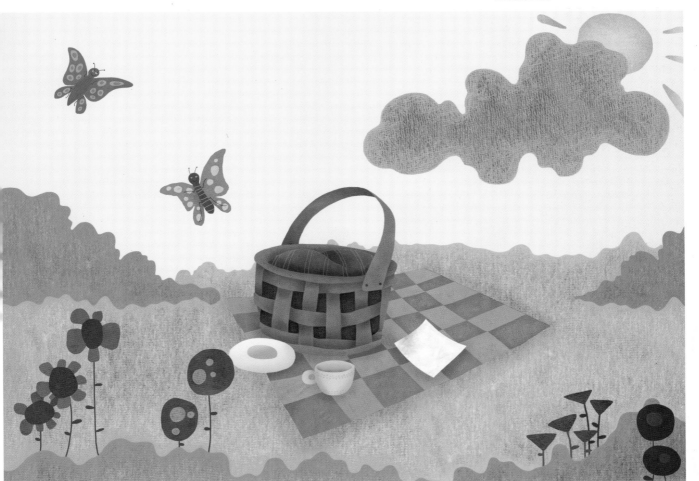

I have a 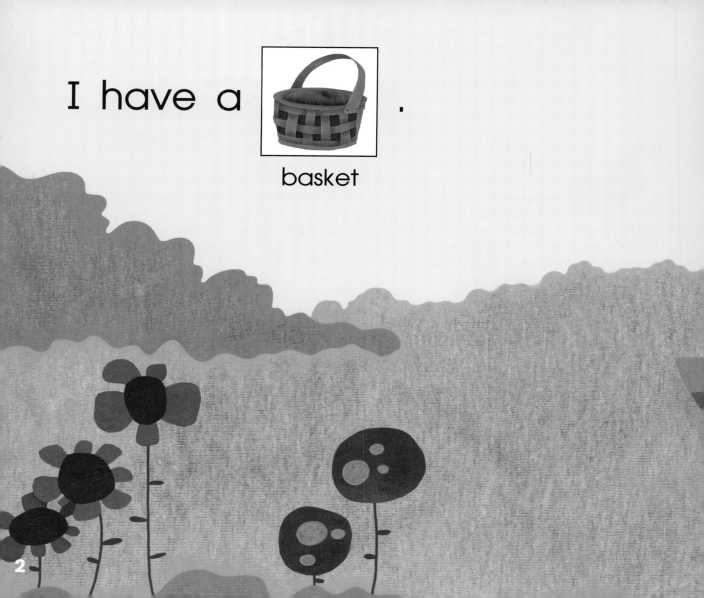 .

basket

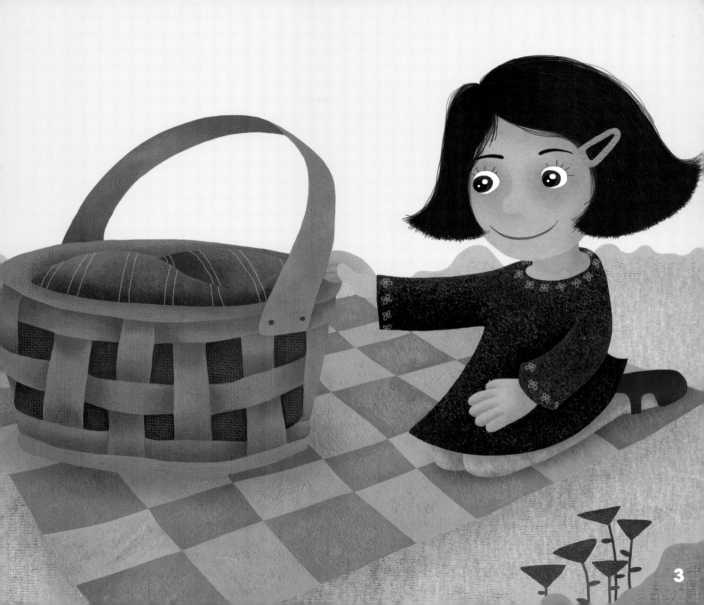

I have a 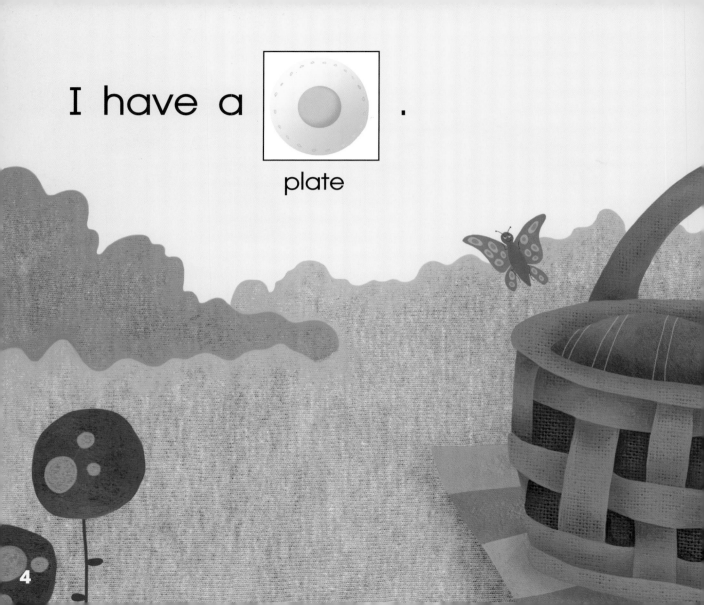 .

plate

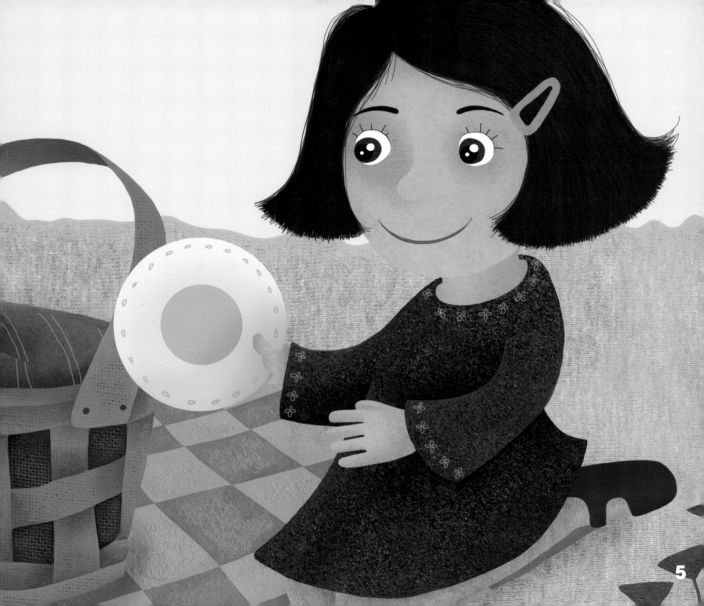

I have a 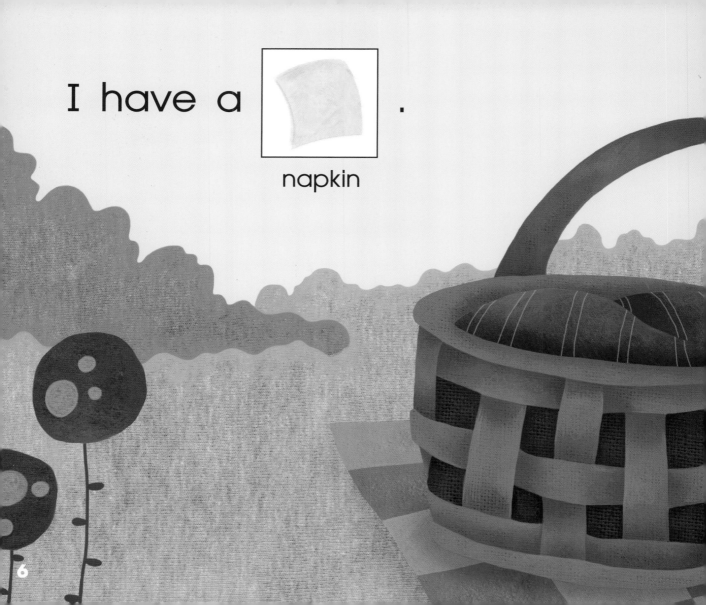 .

napkin

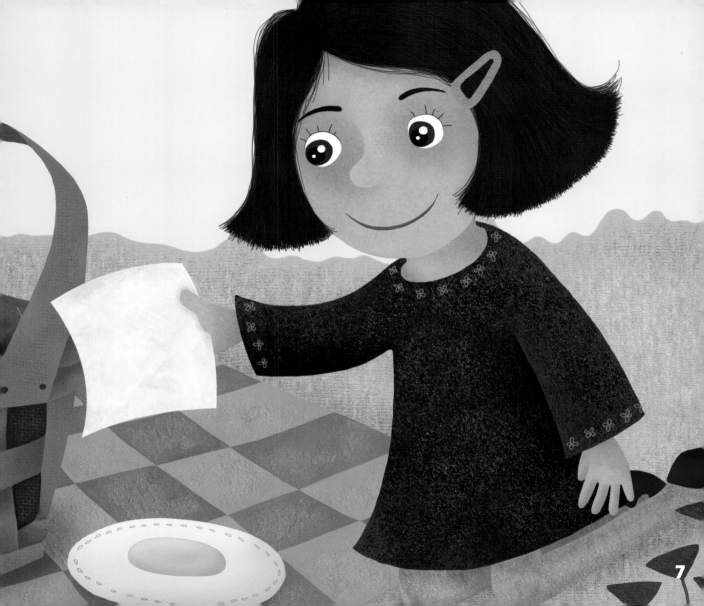

I have a 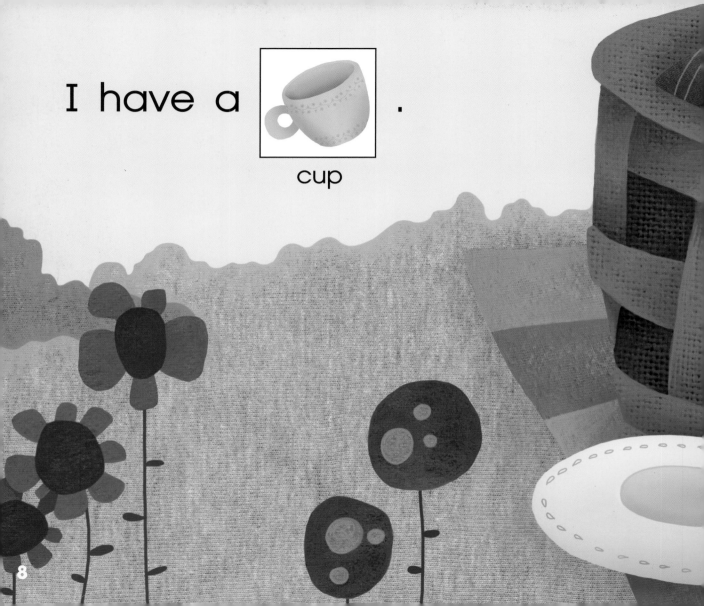 .

cup

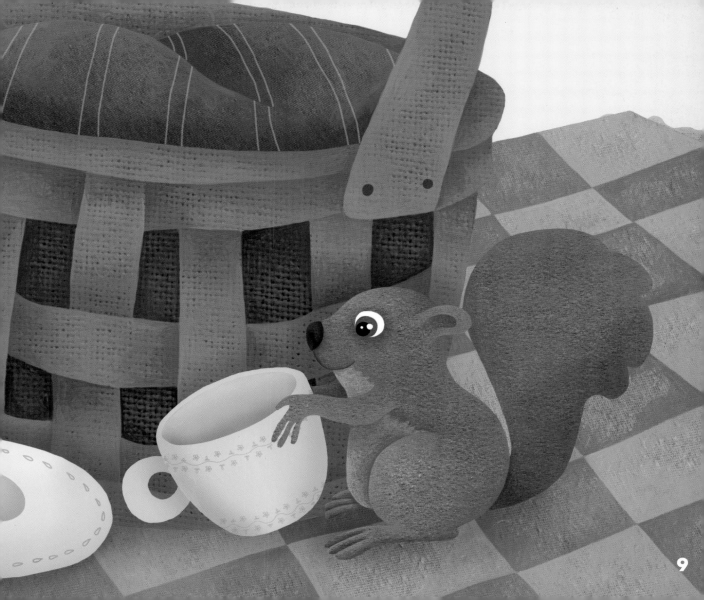

I have a 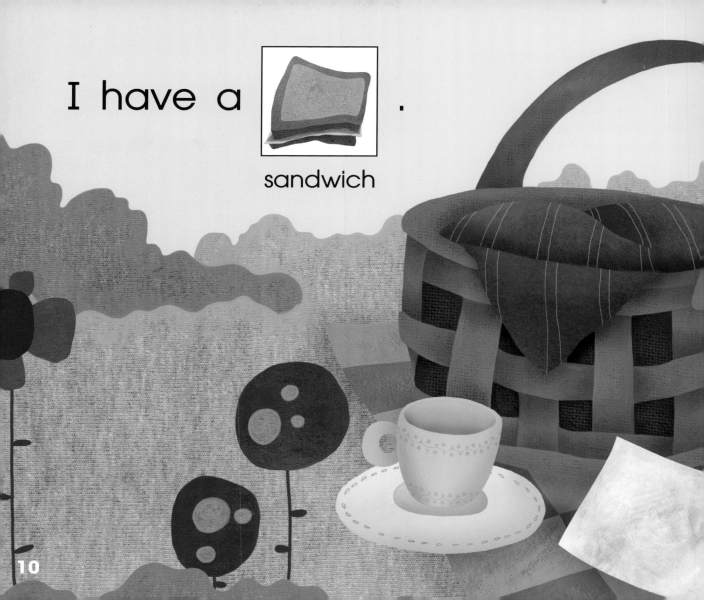 .

sandwich

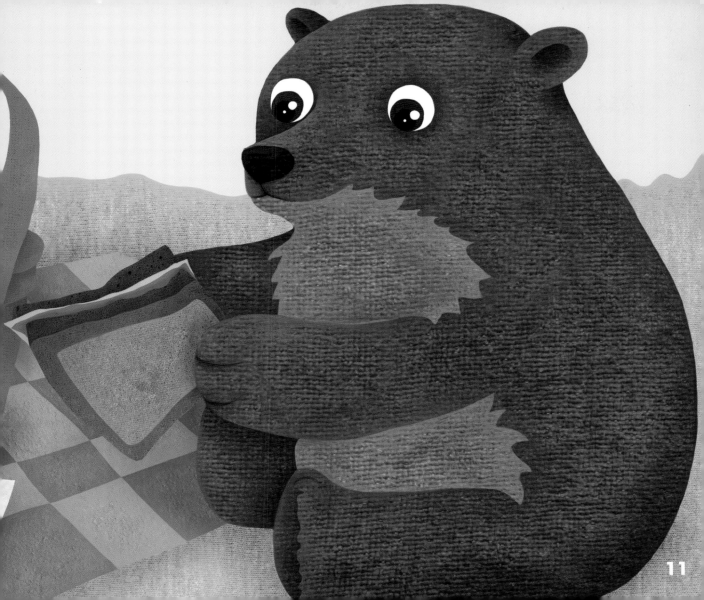

I have a 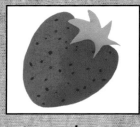 .

strawberry

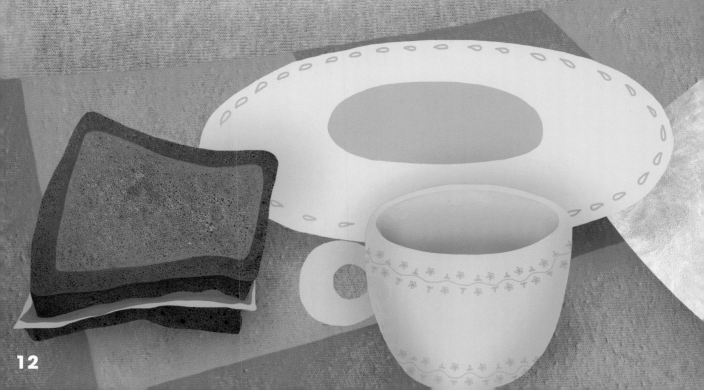

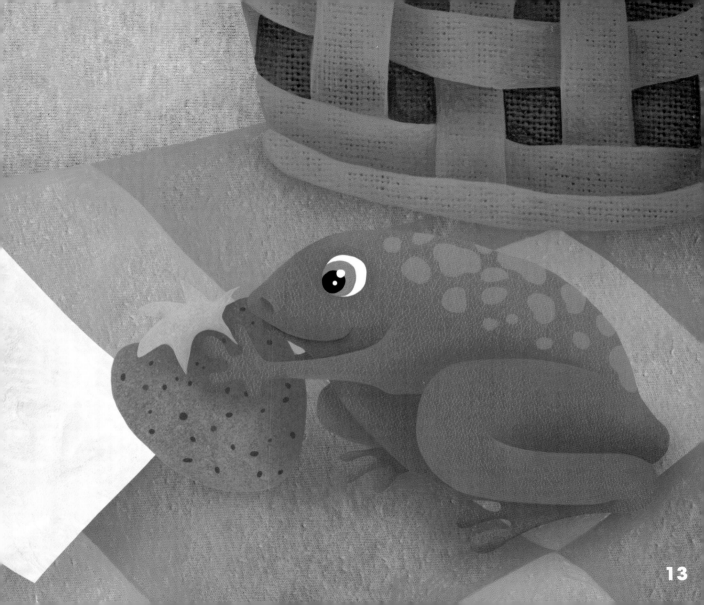

I have a 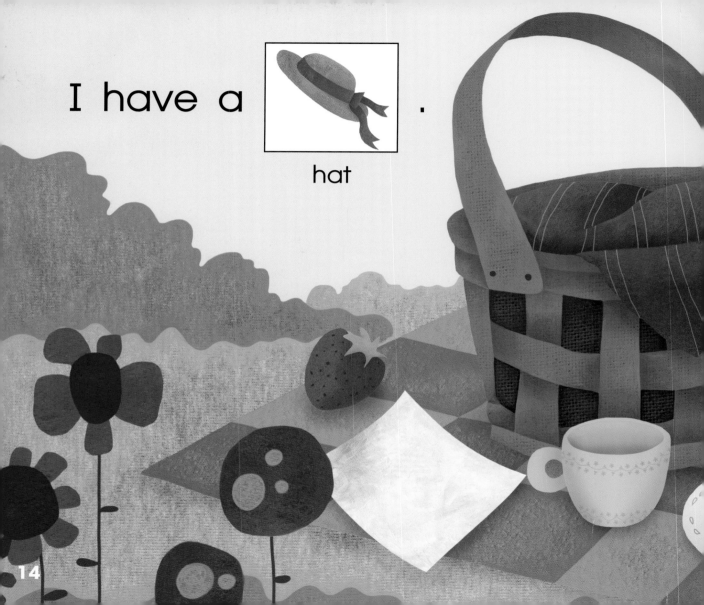 .

hat

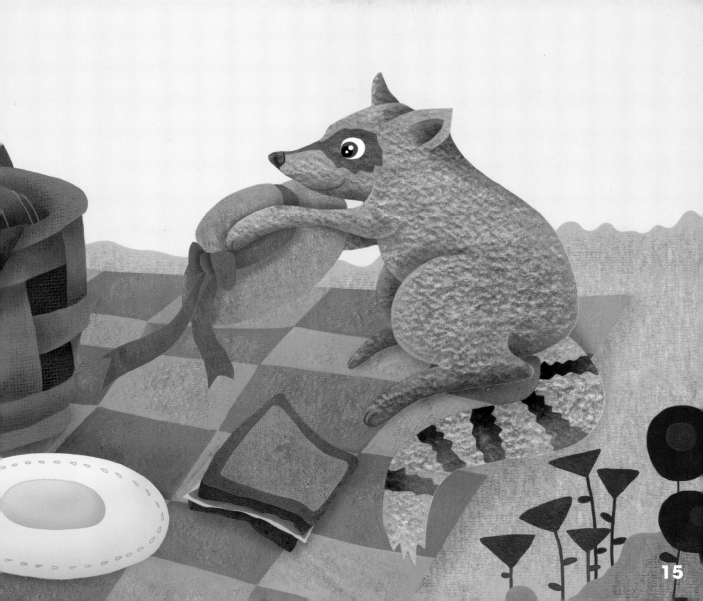

I have a 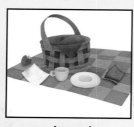 .

picnic

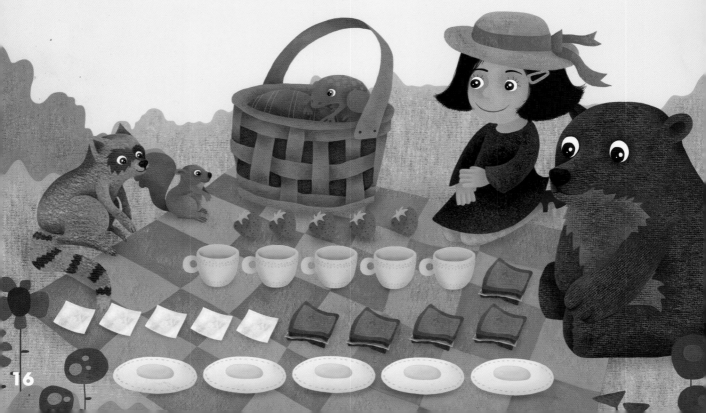